Seeing

where love happens that lasts
for forever

Todd Brady de Garcia
@toddymanners

for each of my siblings

individually and

together with you

with love

for today

and forever

love,
Todd the Frog

breath

living for
another
day
to be
✡ here
inside
of
a poem

breath

living for
another
day
to be
☆ here
inside
of
a poem

today
is
everything.

Table of Contents

- - - - - - - - - = poem continues

_________ = poem complete

- - - - - - - - - = poem continues

__________ = poem complete

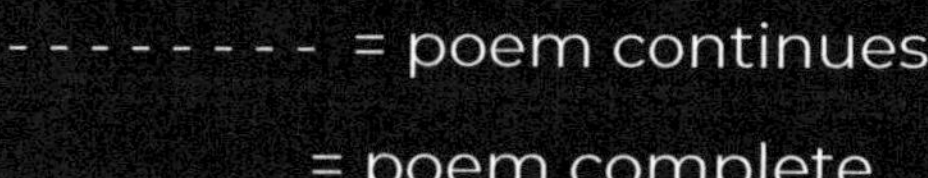

- - - - - - - - = poem continues

___________ = poem complete

- - - - - - - - = poem continues

__________ = poem complete

... and Jesus saith
unto his rainbow crew,
don't worry about
people who spit my name
at you; they don't know
what the fuck they're talking about.
I got you; we are
all the way
fam ♡

_.305.x25._

twenty five
three sixty fives
found

worth living
for twenty four hours

at a time,
not hiding from

believing,
even in me;

denying none of those days

their
one
chance
of experiencing
another
impossible

miracle.

a way

to be here

       is my favorite part

of being.

twenty four hours at a time,

one year from today

will look both different and the same while still growing every which-way.

4/24/24

4

ain't nothin' to see
∘ — ∘ — ∘

when you shine a penlight
        or one of those fancy
high-powered bright-beams
            into the wide
opened eyes of what is misnamed
        christianity, you will see
all the way at
    the very back, the last midnight
    routes of retina-railroad
tracks...that... won't ...ever... detach
from homophobia's home base. An"other"
wide-open "field of freshly threshed
visions, already wired-up in hay bales
like there is nothing left to do that's
beyond shifting; new storage. old,
unused souls, lifted up and measured
in stacked centimeters that will not;

        change any of this until
everything begins coming together.

Anonymous.

suiting up

and showing up

remembering that

we

are only doing today.

Welcome Home

another day of making
what's large

tiny

enough

to see,

and

what's

tiny

large

enough

for the

display

of invisible breathing

found in unhurried

beauty...

7

4124

TsdG

be one of those people
who people get mad at
when you stand up and
disagree.
be
one of those
people who people stomp their feet at,
as loudly as they can,
making jumping beans out of old
resting pebbles
when you are one who gazes at them,
inquisitively, with clear eyes, be one
of those
blasphemous people who say
things
that herd-mentality ...likes...to enforce...
silence about thinking
through gaslit interrogation, that
useful, useless intimidation; you,
please be
one of those people who already know that
we
will never
go into hiding in order
to
be.

blending bubbles

everyone and anybody else
        sometimes breathe
exactly the same breath
        just like two
scuba divers together when
one's
tanks
run out of O2; there's no question.

            that
    slow ascent

        of   matching

                    velocities,

        with

            our

                rising

    mutual
        bubbles;
                        saving us both.

blind obedience

trafficking
in soul violence;
hatred makes entitlement claims while
drawing from clear, decision-free buckets,
refilled with group-thought's refreshing
cold-truths directly reflected from
the "One Plus One Equals Two" true-source;
Deeply True Love, God's warmth
        kept holy, inside
poisoned wells for the parched; those
golden ladles, overflowing
        with gurgling judgment. Sating
blood thirst (assuredly not from satan).
it's not wrong, when acting
on behalf of everyone, for everyone; it's
just us here, preparing
for the second coming of God's holy
smoking gun. Someone said God said
true devotion dictates
let it be so.

blind rage

there's nothing
that can't be re-made
into a weapon. stuck
serving time living
a musical cliché
still here,
year after year
in somebody else's prison.
yeah, right.
every-single-person
    singing the same music,
        mis-judged blood in a chorus
claiming we're all innocent
individuals; it's just that
someone else's words got trapped
in our endless sentences.
what is left to learn
        if not
                stuff like
                        how to make a
shank
out of anything

just twisting junk up
with some heat.
my own, handmade,
beautiful serrated blade,
stiff duct-taped handle
made for holding what's mutual:
hefty levels of blind rage
just waiting. quick muscles
collapse your eyes

    Mmmppf!!
    Mmmppf!!
    mmmppf!
    Mmmppf.

    finally,

all done.

blind spot

—₀—₀—₀—

white-knuckled on another
heart-racing rage-freeway,
doing quick-swerves into
blinker-free squeeze-throughs
high-speed lane-jumps;
check your blind spot to be sure
you don't see

Jesus,
riding his motorcycle,
helmet-free, right there, with his sparkling
warm smile and flying hair, hoping
that he's not just about to be
creamed
by another
true believer.

the blind shall see

trusting another's vision to include you
when you can't see on your own is next to
impossible; that blind trust
only comes once
there are   no other options
left open.   the fruit
looking like poison, held
im front   of you to consider if
there   isorisnt
anything   else anything   left anything
you can   trust   ;
that first   taste   of nectar
cooling   your   cracked throat, then
maybe.

21424

chest thumpers are gonna
wanna getta combustible
chest thumper and
touchie feelies are gonna
wanna get that more fuzzy,
customary one who understands
how to be convincingly
complimentary, just
get that scratch right while
the scattered and can't
decide who what or where
they care to buzz about
in 5, 4, 3, 2, the done will stand by...
keeping count as everyone sings
together, another round of
"follow my simple directions"
their erections harmonizing with
a one and a two and a
"see, I told you so". those good ol'
a cappella
standards in
unison; then...
the swinging sword fights begin.
3225

definition is
different than
pre-destination
no matter
who
tells you what or who
you
already are;
right
here.

____

16

a demagogue disappears
without someone,
anyone
to rule over and push

down, but even
completely on their own,
transgender humans will remain
exactly
who
they
are

no matter who else is around.
So; who is
truthfully
the stronger human of the two
is not
in question.
318225

17

did you forget

or was that

leave me alone.

do you ever wonder
how much of what you find
        un/acceptable
is just because somebody thought
   for a second or a minute or for
      more than a few moments a million
        years ago, for whatever reason,
that THAT is the way to be, without
   anyone worrying or wondering about why
      THAT should be; or how
                    THAT matters for some
maybe made-up reason, meaning
            that THAT
is automatically so matter-of-fact still today?
yeah; neither had anyone.
no wonder jumping up
      to question anything
         about exactly   → THAT, ←
freaks the fuck outta anyone outside of freaks,
   who retain ALL power,
      by just glaring back and
         whispering a menacing BOO!

19 ______________

driving,____.off-road

watch people go wall-eyed
when you're not on automatic
about their
be-on-the-same-page stuff;
disagreeing, even peacefully, with
whatever their "there-it-is", is.
we already know what to do
to save our own souls; off-road.
there's a whole lot more to this
seriousness. our playtime on earth,
seeing what fits into this book-bag.
blank paper
portraits of propaganda ghosts
wearing invisible
false mustaches, right next to this
flip-top-box of sixty-four-colors
with a built-in sharpener.
imagine that.
like it had all been pre-made
with everything in exactly the right place
for running this whitewashing act
clean off of the page.

everything is a poem
when you were born with
the eyes of a poet
who sees that
everything has its very own
        ...incredible...yet,
indescribable butterfly-words arriving
here again
with a brain-rattling, still-wordless rhythm
that is immediately indelible. you must
try to describe every wing-pedal
before you die
because, just because; just...
maybe you...
are or were or will be the only
one
who saw what you know
you did; exquisite, openly porous
visions with impeccable rhythm ...that...
bouncing and bouncing and bouncing
all through your gyrating head
saying pretty please,
with your own human voice, my sweet,
pick up your pen.

for the record

as I write this,
the government is turning
against my beautiful wife and me.
our family,
siempre juntos y siempre cresciendo
law abiding citizens who need
to make emergency   escape
                          plans

yes, really.
you see
this is
what happens when
your own country makes you its enemy;
    points at you from the TV
    saying
    scary scary scary you can't be
    herewith
    normal people.

giving focus to e v e r y t h i n g
that
I hope to do   with love
and
greatness, is like writing new poems
two feet
away
from
Flea,
playing his happy bass while

jumping up and down, all smiles and
pure recklessness

on top of Vincent Van Gogh's

bouncy mattress.

God must be laughing, sometimes,
not at us, but
at the way that we
sometimes like to talk
with that one voice we only use
while we are praying
in front of others.
Not in a making fun of us way;
more in a "why
 are you talking to me
like I don't know you, or like
I'm some Martian Diplomat
with dark sunglasses on
who could just as easily snap
you in half as give you
half now half later all of those
whole golden kingdoms
but only if you posture-yammer like
you're an overpaid television news anchor
using that one voice
you would never use
anywhere else. Mad respect
                          is found

inside of your actions, my homie,
way more than your phoney channel 4
ten o'clock weather report tone."
God must be laughing at that,
sometimes,
thinking, Dude, it's me; don't talk to me
like we don't know each other
better than anyone else who knows
everything
good bad and oddly hilarious
about you,
like that voice of a weird stranger
you sometimes use when you're talking

to me

about
everything that's important

between us.

greatness
     be what is
already;
all-ready-here with
        everything whether
invisible
        or just unseen... you
              reach
as you have from where

you were to where you are

      to where
        you will be all

                    at once.

____

26

gut compass.

hearing bou, while you look at me
the same way
as every other time that I felt
this way
saying
"it's not what you think "
solidified
confirmation.
what I knew wasn't
a feeling.

how to escape a fake incubator

just another incidental life

precious
beneath
dialed-in
precision-heat
 stabilization;
the perfect day set to begin
pecking and stretching
against the inside of
stuccoed protection
knowing
 those thin, inner-walls are meant
to be busted through
some timeless day...

such elegant design
                    —though

not always so
                entirely capable
        to suss
    out on its own
    what cannot be allowed
                    to connect

tissue to soul; removal
from delicious

        heat-lamp warmth, not worthy;

    de
        gen

    er
    a

                        shun ...

dont-tell-me-what-isn't-kept
intact,

                stubborn soul;
here for this
interruption-attempt
face-off with fetid dogmas
thinking
they're deciding, again,
what should be

                        left
            fetid...
                    cold

confusion grows its own membrane

of capable
songs of holiness,
still
yearning
to be learned
word-for
all-of-those-joyful

words singing
through
insistent
tree branches
seeing every horizon
escalated;
my lungs filled with
sweet
sweet
oxygen
my own
insistent life
from earth's
tip-tops
safe now
beneath more
comprehensible
warning lamps of
generational conversations between
true sunlight and genuine earth.

continuity happens

    to sing

                  --- 4 ----

that one, promised song,
containing so much greatness it begs

both you and me

for every note we both know

must be
motherfucking sung out loud
...this... one... time...

then
again

        and again

                and again...

————————————

I am a beautiful woman
who
you won't know is
            beautiful
until you know how
to see me, and before you
        are even able
            to see me standing
before you, know
you mustn't worry about me
wondering if you will ever see
...me,
for I will;
and I will know... that
I am a beautiful woman.

                    For Nikki Giovanni ♡

I was certain
   that this was just the new face
      of everyone who would always hate
         more than enough of me before knowing
even the first truth about me.

Certain of the fact that
   I would always be   that stain
            that wouldn't
         go away, chasing away what I didn't
want to stay, then begging please stay

all the way gone. I was certain that
   what felt good would
            hurt me, either quickly or slowly,
               because
nothing could be trusted

again, especially when they say
        "of this,
            you can be certain." I was certain
    that this was the time that
            I really was going to remain
                    depressed as fuck
for the rest of my life because I was
                            certain

        that that one thing
        that was legit killing me
            was also the only thing left
            that I could rely on to keep me alive,
motherfucking certain

        that I was done
with God,
            and with everyone, and that
        God was all the way done with me
        too.
    certain from both ends of worthlessness,

— — —2— — — — —

wanting nothing

            right up to the day
          that I found out;

I was certainly wrong.

it was never about the harpooning

it hadn't ever been
a fore-
or afterthought
before my first time;
penetrated
by someone
older, when
under-aged.
once the question of why
had been loosened up by
instructions... and poppers
just a finger at first,
gentle with don't try to understand
just let yourself
fall into the feeling in
slo-mo
I didn't know
people like me
do this,
with or without spit;
loosened up at
sweet-ass sixteen, wanting
to go back and...

just... say...

your name never mattered
and even if you had asked,
you'd get my fake one; yes,

I am old enough.

just this morning

I stopped mid-stride and I

could;

here.

5725

looking and seeing are siblings
who,
similar to
two other well-named
relatives,
listening and hearing,
can go years
without having
anything to do with each other.
all of that
realness is
their own story
to tell or not tell,
whereas this
indisputable witness
is owned in its wholeness;
all on its own
without any need for anything
more familial.
just taking a moment
to be seeing.

did you ever hear anything
starting with "they say" that turned out
to be true; harmless mirth mixed with
measureless dismissiveness
merely a manipulation to sell tickets,
they say. in a poetry slam
your score...is not...your poem.
that random patron's measurement is just
a parlor game stacked to gain
large crowds wanting to see competition when
everyone
was born from that one
sperm-swimmer who found a way
to win.
who decided that there was more
deciding to do
by some outside swimmers?
this was not their hundred meters
to feed...merely warmed;
deep waters muscled through cupped hands
pulling strong currents back with a double kick
to the next ready egg that's mine to find,
with another
motherfucking ten.

My poems are not cutesy.
They don't rhyme the right way
and they don't only convey
warmth; poems of love and semi-precious stuff.
You may not find any poems, in fact,
like the poems that
you're used to. They're probably not poems
for church or for grandma or for anyone
who is hoping to not feel
like they've been punched in the face,
but instead,
want to feel all happy inside;
still on-course once they've reached the end.
These are the poems for people who feel
like the not-happy already happened,
at the ending before the beginning. Punched-
out, knocked off-course right in front of
everyone, and everyone
deciding to awkwardly look away,
trying to find something that looked
a little bit more, how shall we say;
cutesy.

not just
you had better not let me hear you
say "just"
as your first word
describing anything about
who you are
what you do and
how you add
    to the human,
    group photograph of
greatness.
don't worry;
    I will remind you (more than once
    if that becomes necessary),
    while you're learning
    how to drop-kick that word
far far away from who you are,
    for good, although please
don't make me have to say it again.

one bird

do you think
    that this bird
is not meant to sing
        unless
        this
        one
        bird
        Sings
the same way
as all of the other birds in the trees?

for one hundred and one
billion years
nothing was wasted,

when I became
multicolored, suddenly
breathing here

now...

and once

I am

in my season of leaving,
I will
decompose
...into nothing

being wasted
...again...

otherwise

everyone
is worth loving.
not just sort of, but,
being loved
deeply, with the kind of love
that doesn't matter
if anyone
agrees "to gift" that love with
their irrelevant validity;
when every molecule of being is alive
breathing-singing-exclaiming
dancing-laughing
        creating
something of Beauty
  Anew
from exoskeleton's
futile struggle
to stop
nature
from splitting-open
                ...and sighing.
bone-level vitality
via
  any smaller understanding,

most strenuous efforts
of trying to convince
Love

of some

false significance
of anything that speaks
                    otherwise;

you have got to be kidding.

remind me.
you're who, again?

Paying attention is the same thing
    in meaning
        as Tuning-in with
        not needing to understand
anything about
        anything
        that doesn't matter,
when
        just being present

for
        Everything,
        is Everything.

already standing on two feet;
        her Eyes
So Openly Beautiful
        locked directly on mine

knowing
   we Belong Together

breathing...
   within our
   shared
      Sanctuary... we are

both

   ;

   our very own.

perfectly imperfect people

you know that that
"nobody's perfect" cliché
is perfectly true,
right?
You do?
Good,
because
there's a little bit more to that,
than that.
Here's the trick,
and stay honest with me
about this.
We would have an impossible time
finding anyone
who is completely terrible
or completely good.
That just doesn't exist.
Ever.
Admit that now or start over
at the beginning of the poem until you
see the need to.

'cause honesty right...
or why are we talking 'cause Jesus
weren't no liar.

now, here's the thing, for real,
once we get that honesty at least
part-way breathing.
scale the fuck outta that shit;

actually (big word warning)
concatenating

every subset of any population into
"All of Those (fill in the slurred-blank)"
of anyone and still say you're... right...
when you c'aint be sure
you and all of yourn
ain't the wrong goods,
god-fearin'
not bad or at all
evil, good 'ol boys who
just caint cut that bullshit sniff-test
out, honestly,
any longer.

pet peep number two:
"I love that for you"
sounding as if
there is just

the tiniest twitch

of subconscious or
passive-aggressive

condescension. I get it.

What grew for me
was not for you;
no duh. It wasn't supposed to be

for you.

You can go ahead
and split on-outta here while

I get along;

all the way
back to my happy.

plagiarizing poems

How could I do anything
other than default
into my high-school-lock-brain when
assigned to write wannabe poetry
 for the first time
for my honors English class.
Fucking poetry.
Fuck that.
Finishing a sectional Shakespeare
together, knowing
our poetry-pushing teacher would choose
the same five Golden Students
she always stuck (her stuck-up self) with
as clear examples
of scholarly perfection,
reading their pearl drops aloud.
Every gasp hocking-up
witticisms struck wise with
perfectly timed smile-shrugs;
truth and ingenuity
all wrapped in one and

sponsored here today by our good friends:
deep dimples,
perfect teeth,
and sparkling clean storm drains.
So naturally,
I just plagiarized Rush.
The only music worth listening to
in high school; choosing
a song that I knew
my lip-clenched instructor
would never know.
I plagiarized the fuck out of it.
Word-for-word; all of that perfect structure
completely intact, and still,
she had not found it to be
quite   (or not to be-hah!)
top-tier enough
to exceed the gorgeous talent
of her golden five. Who knew.
Had I decided
that her opinion had mattered
idabeen stuck,
like whatever student
was up her butt.

- - - 2 - - - -

Know this, my dear high schoolers:
you have my explicit
written permission
to plagiarize
the whiz-bang fucking-shit out of anything
that I have ever written, if you want to.
Signed, me.
It likely won't help you to "get an A",
at least not every time,
but it could-maybe help you
to get through
one more idiotic day of stupid-ass
F'd-up high school,
with a hidden smile or two;
even if that means borrowing a few
of mine for a little while.
PEACE, my homeroom homie.
(space here for doodling when you're bored.)

55

popping with rhythm

no matter what, that writer
won't let me sleep a full night.
kicking my feet with rude restless
rhythms relentlessly cutting
            that hard line
ahead of my alarm clock again.
telling my important, deep bones with
its most serious tones that time only exists
to get busy with
whatever is standing here
spanking your bare-bitch-ass butt-cheeks
today (not always in a bad way)

and here I am;

listening like a good boy...
reliable pen and paper present,
with hand prints,
all popping with rhythm again.

prayerfulness, sorta like
long sentences of swear words you
only say in secret
        holy places; then, forgiveness
singing hallelujah in a chorus with
all of my lightning bug friends
    flying through this beautiful
        storm... finally,

just that.

pruning

echoing all of that nonsense
again; I should have
already
lit the match. that nasty, burning
leftover odor does not have to
remain generational
when
the only way to continue
growing at all
is to just
burn it all down.

58

rain does not follow desire
   the way of cigarettes
settling into a mutual calming
      of what has already been sated
          rain evaporated first;
prepared itself
   to quench a thirst that was

                                        born
   before the earth knew
   to bring

                          the two of us

          together.

for : Drew

59   __________

(don't). Say. gay. _

saying that God is the reason that you
had to either harass
or turn your backs
on all of those faggots
is the deadliest form of perfunctory
bullshit, so keep your
homo-hating church-version of LOVE
in the over-stuffed crawl-space of
your faith's opaqued brain where
your ignored humanity gets shoved; just
blame that stuff on birthright supremacy
secured through generationally
performative piousness; insistent with the
sincerity that always accompanies feeling
better than all others. Owning the truth
includes the privilege of ignoring
responsibility
to personally own Any of That. Instead just
stuck with the grunt-work of herding
one day-a-week congregations of sheep
shaking out tithes and trying
        to get your lonely halo
            outta the pawn shop.
    - - - - 1 - - - -

fake-Afraid of Catching AIDS (remember lepers?)
through direct eye contact
just shuffle personal "minor infractions" off
with a shrug, claiming any blame for
     cutting people off
                              was somehow
out-of-your-hands due to imitation-scriptural
               sin; making LAWS of the LAND
     making it a CRIME to say the word "Gay",
to welcoming cheers from Church Houses
                         Everywhere; their
Self-Righteous-Steeples-Spread-Countrywide
Showing Gay-People-of-Every-Age that
God-Holds-No-Refuge for All of Those Fornicators
parading about in their jock straps and feathers
with that Heinous Heart Condition they call LOVE.
Insisting on Inflicting what's
     Inherently Disgusting onto others; onto
     God's-True-Believers Busy with
     Preaching from Bent Pulpits to
"Keep on stuffing that Perverted shit into the
dark corners As Far Away As It Can Get from
God's Chosen Clique." I just gotta ask...

          ---- 2 -----

What happened to gay lives matter
the way that black lives are supposed to?
Who is our community's Breonna or Philando,
          and who, please tell me, is
our Eric, trying to say "I can't breathe"
I'll tell you this:
the reason that this remains a mystery
is that "our people" don't get strangled or shot
by bigots or police
                    (at least not as often).
Our community's Travon, is not getting shot
for wearing a black hoodie, ours is
          just another
          anonymous teenager
                    shooting himself for being
thought of as too light in the loafers.
Our community's George cannot breathe...
because of having his soul strangled...
          ...by the people who he loves
until he hangs himself in his
                    air-tight closet.
People can't say their names because
     nobody knows them, because
     every single one of them

- - - 3 - - -

felt like they had died in shame, while
most of their families would agree with them.
Stealing their own lives from themselves and
        life partners
        if they had even
        lived long enough to find one.
Find our names.
    Say them out loud until you know them.
thirteen: too young to have ever known
        the feeling of not being alone.
    seventeen: "is that a boy or a girl?
        who knows, just throw rocks at it".
    twenty-five: without a first or last name
        that mattered either.
    thirty-two: a former missionary, like me,
        pinning a sign on himself,
        saying "DO NOT RESUSCITATE", walking
        to the front steps of his church
                !!!BANG!!!
            ...parents... saying...
        "that's what you get
when you choose   that lifestyle."

63   ----- H - - -

...and, in case =YOU= felt like you were done
   ...with reading a "list"...
thirty-eight: joining thousands of
   pushed-aside nobodies and
forty-one: finding it better to be found
   in a body-bag
   than in the arms of a loving man.

But not this guy.
Getting all the way to sixty-two by
   STANDING MY GROUND while stubbornly
STILL BREATHING not leaving RED-HANDED,
   just LIVING with LOVE, long enough, to hear
   the Government tell Everyone that
WE-MUST-BE-VERY-careful to
   Not Violate Any Laws
   when talking about all of the
   DEAD DEAD DEAD DEAD DEAD
      → being extra sure ←
      to not say
      the word
      GAY
      ----- s -----

... just in case

anyone

who is considered

vulnerable

is listening.

self-ownership setting sail

those times that you Can't
figure out the Big stuff like
How
         the holy Fuck
                  to Talk to people
     or with people
                       or to just
adjust and be present
     with people
                  when you know you are
in that one spot that ain't able to get
Going Anywhere Else; screaming
     Inside Voice needing to Go
Outside of these places where
   Everyone Else Knows what they're doing;
...like now... leaving everything to sink
into my book with a pen where anywhere,
     in any moment,
I can be fluent
     with who I am; breathing
                    again.

Shadrack and Purple Church of Jesus
get it together with
their experiential lineage; that just
seems like a heavy lift.
Generations of stories, the adventurous
jizz of collective DNA sewn together by
highways of unlikely one-person-begats
cemented to unknown destinations,
thousands of mind-lightyears from where
any of these current situations'
thought-anscestors began.

All of those what ifs got stuffed into storage
containers labeled "didn't" and "did"
while what is and what may become
keep getting busy with making more babies.

Shadrach, my wild man,
meet Purple Church of Jesus.
Neither of you could have
ever been here and
somehow
both of you already is.

<u>shifting down</u>
caught in my busy brain
I stop
for long enough

      ...to watch
the pace of the clouds,
    with all of their purpose...

        ...Moving
        across the blue
            sky...

  ...for awhile
until my breathing...

...matches theirs;   ...oscillating...
  these clouds...

        ...and me, grinning
      at being...

present.

sound it out

beauty found Mom
in loud laughter
about what she had found
to be much more ridiculous
than serious;

the unrestrained homemade heart of everything
that mattered to me
more than anything.
teaching me how to read and write, then
   to follow-through and do them both

often, and often
   finding both necessary
for my childhood heart
   to breathe, even again; these things
will always be

connected

with the sound of her crying
as far away from everyone as she could get
 without leaving;
howling out the worst parts of her life...
muffled, as best as she could as though

she was face down, sunken
ear-deep in old pillows; the sound of being
on her own again   lost somewhere
in the furthest-back room of our family home.
The livingroom television

going loud
about not knowing
how to pronounce these new words;
like inconsolable,
just

hearing syllables

being sounded out

again.

space dust
went backwards and found out
forty years was not, in fact,
more than a day ago, or established
for long enough
in my brain, yet,
surviving through that day

    ...still...feels...spiked...

with what was
immeasurable
confusion
making me
wonder
did any of all of
that
really
ever happen   when
creativity becomes its own
             generational life-force.

everything and
nothing are both
simultaneously
somehow the same
making my head
snorkle-swim
into wavy dream-murk
data that never
finds truth's anchored grasp
onto what
it's feeling, correctly, left
free-falling
through beaded-curtains on the way
into somewhere
floating cubby-holes
left graffiti'd
when

- - — 2 - - - -

denial of gravity is captured
again...
        safety, back in its proper place,
for a moment
        of even
        drum beats
begging everyone
    to just stop
for long enough
        to queue-up our dying remix and
        blink delicious again...
            inside of these deepening rhythms
            together...
a naked night swim
our own private DJ;
everything

came apart inside time
for my afternoon
disco nap.
did anybody all the way die?

nothing
still being
resolvable is
gonna maybe make it
tougher
to see all of our holy relics
          as they have remained
               as alive as we are

integral
puzzle pieces - connecting us - just
   'cause -

          all of this

               is
               sacrosanct

                    space dust...

               FUck
               AIDS

speaking what goes unspoken

Our great protectors will help us
to not be exposed
to dangerous stuff, like
drag queens reading story books
about cartoon penguins
having two papas,
bunnies who wear bow ties,
or kids finding their way through
concrete walls of dismissals and
group-disgust delivering
predictably ubiquitous
you-don't-belong-here missives;

just

dont-kill-yourself.

hatred.
it's clearly the only way
to safety.

schooling kids with the correct
meanings of things
by burning every book
about weirdos like me, who
    wear bow ties, who you
don't or didn't or do always keep
        a secret... trap-door
easily within arms' reach, but only
for clarifying doctrinally
how to understand
how critically important it is
to be fully on-board with this
one-version-of-things, exactly
like everybody who hates me.
 Attention! Today's only lesson:
light this bonfire and eradicate
    all of those villainous others
        even if it means that we must
courageously
continue to light our own hair on fire.

      = queer books save lives =

Stonewall was a Riot

You don't get to remove our history.
Even you, pretending to be a king
who pooped his pants and called it
executive policy; fuck you.
Yeah, you don't get to do that.

Do you think that human beings just begin
throwing bricks and bottles, because they
became bored with nothing left to do; due to
not being left to be anything other than
those queens and faggots who riot?
Well, you're right.

When you have been shown to be and been kept
at less than nothing, again and again,
by everyone from fire snorting preachers
to contestants of beauty pageants to
your own mom and dad, you know that
reaching...for nothing... is reaching up...to

what they thought they saw: crimes of God;
less as just donning assless chaps with
   a prayer of invocation, as lit up, born for
   throwing back shots with bites of lime then
   all perfectly manicured hands on deck, to
   throw molotov cocktails at our oppressors;
those uniformed protectors of conformity
                              and peace.

Marsha P. Johnson and Sylvia Rivera
             live forever
you beautiful
       exiled transexuals
leading us into the exhileration of
          "no longer."

no snack-cracker-dusted-twat has any power
to remove
     any of your history, your ferocity, your
       sheer panty-hosed courage, bravely
         bonzai-kicking motherfucking bullshit
all the way into outer space with its obituary
super-glued to its shit-stained forehead.

- - - — ² - - - - -   78

Dedicated to:

Marsha P. Johnson and Sylvia Rivera
and every person who they have inspired,
unapologetically representing

the capital Letter T
in LGBTQIA+

right from the very beginning.

Stonewall Riots NYC, June 28, 1969

plus one heartfelt honorable mention
for the beautiful man
who smooshed a pie, right in the face, of
that orange juice shillin' pageant contestant.

80

Sunset park at sunrise with my buddy,
AppleJacks both of us wearing
  gray muzzles, he walks
   faster than me, but
we are both able
to find enough trees to pee on.

Wherever he's off to, wilding-around
while I stay, on the path I know
that   he is   seeing all of this
as our own wilderness experience. Living
our best life as puppy and papa, forever.
Nothing else would make any sense.

A smiling dog with wide-happy eyes,
finding everything that he can smell
to be more interesting than anything else;
   maybe a bite of that, spit that out
   maybe not, but what is that
     way over there with the rising
     sunlight changing all of its colors.

Never too far from each other
any call-out sound
from either of us will immediately
bring the other over,
to stand or sit or run or discover
every astonishment; just
the two of us, here at sunset park
at sunrise.

Swear Words

Good things to say sometimes become
bad words to use, as if those words have a few
poor morals. Incongruence may have a little
something to do with it, like greased-up
PTSD through the overuse of so many
intentionally abusive misnomers
like

Jesus Christ, once he had finally found a way
to stop tap dancing; snapping into full
commando role, entering a phase of
exclusive hate-privilege knocking-up
big-power-money honey, and of course
wearing matching tri-colored everything,
natch; in order to be showy enough about
Patriotism, being a true blue blood, formulating
cut and paste cultism expeditiously reached
through rabbit-hole lobotomies, turning everyone
into exactly the same political self-serving-self
righteousness, let-sweet-freedom-ring ≡only≡
one-way_to_be_being   only ≡seemingly≡
menacing words meaning...   remember

- - 1 - - -

those Good ol Days that happened, way before
gathering up so dad-gum much impossibly-heavy
woke-baggage; thank God for the servile
brown-nosing-bell-boy showing up, just hoping
for a tap on the head after disposing of
big suitcases bursting with toxic maga colon DEI
now replaced with made-in-China bright-future
Flag-Shaped Lapel-Pins; claiming every single one
of those salutable-beautiful stars and stripes
would no-never confuse narcissism with freedom
without our diamond-clustered-cross-necklaces of
Jesus; these are not mere accessories, this is all
beautifully-inspired-perfect-branding for
the White Man who needs adoration the most.
That televised chanting amidst huge photogenic
crowds, so very patriotic. just look at 'em all, with
their memorized insults and alphabet letters.
pure heartland folk, using everyday words
that celebrate freedom and equality's
desecration; melting it down in a hot,
constitution-free cauldron, then
shaping it all into a cudgel
'cause 'murka,
filled with God's good people who would never
even think of
using ugly swear words.

Sweet Salvation

Long after removing the annoying residues
left after pulling religion's
dogma wedgies
outta my behind, there was this
life saving realization
standing up
from a coulda-forgotten corner
of my cobwebbed mind;
waving at me, in a friendly way, saying
"hey, I think that you kinda know me!"
Of course.
That vaguely familiar
part of my spirit-brain that could still think
about Jesus;
      my Halo'd J, my BFFFE
without realizing out loud in my spirit-brain
that I never think about him
in the past tense, just like
I never think of him ever
being either dead or never alive.
He is always alive in my mind while

I'm thinking about him.
Making that connection again
is maybe
the a-ha of why
I also never think about people
who I love who have died,
as having died
all the way dead, like forever.
I just don't have a place for any of that
in my
spirit-brain. I'll bet that this
endlessness in a good way
is somewhat why it's not a surprise
that people still sing

      Halleluja;

just like this one
sometimes isolated,
  semi-fucked-up kid, saying
"Hey, my sweet Halo'd J.
It's super-good to see you again.
I am very happy that we have re-connected."
Nobody can take that from me;
not even with their stupid wedgies.

tater tot casserole

non-linear or non-
    binary or both what
does it matter when...
    all of the necessary
    ingredients are
accounted for; the present,
accountable.
                those held
beneath conventional broilers
    know the combination
        is within the melting;
just how it becomes
just so.

<u>ten seconds of grace</u>

knowing what letters feel like in your hands
while writing tactile thoughts in the dark
makes it easier to un-see
everything you bring up to let go,
except when it comes to those
goddammit-already poetry-slam timers
interrupting your flow with that same
                    age-old battle:
Essential Components of This vs. It Don't Matter.
fists held Up,
Signaling the Beginning of your
Grace-time Countdown.
Ten Seconds Left to Be
saying Everything that Must-Still-Be-Said;
Eyes closed, just like when
            this was written in the dark
                            that released,
                                    sweet

Fuck it...
    blowing past that blasted
            three-minute timer again.

Ten years out
from the happiest day of my life
when so much
   of what
      I couldn't see then   is still
   here with me now,   just like
everything already was   everyday
upon meeting each other,   already
   flying
         through our mutual
            multi colored universe.
I thought... back then...
   that I had married a very beautiful man
   when in fact, I had
         married a very beautiful woman.
We both rolled along with all of our love
   the way that love does together
   regardless of what had been
   new planets were now found here;
perennial; somehow, both of us
   landing happier here
now   than I ever had been as this
one on the happiest day of my life.

Thank you
    for this new day.
Thank you
      for
    my life
        for my family
          for our beautiful
              home life together
Thank you.

Thank you for helping me
    to finally
    let go of always needing
        to
        compulsively put two and two
        together in that one,
                belonging slot.

Thank you
    for the years
    and years
    and years when I would not
    call you by name but you
        never left me; anyway.

Thank you.

90

That thing (so far)
when you know that you are
the real deal; not at all fake
at the same time that you know
for a fact that
you are doing exactly
that thing that you want to be doing
the very most
with all of this
beautiful wildness.
Yeah.
Reach for that.
It's pretty fucking badass
to know that
you matter-of-factually are
    bonerfied by life doing
in realtime, exactly what
    you stuck with what
you genuinely love what
    you were born to do
    and that this is your
motherfucking time, right now,
                to do all of it.

you will know it when you get here 'cause
your arms

will suddenly be covered

with goosebumps that don't know for sure
how they got there and how or if
they'll ever go away; and
even
if you cannot physically see
any of them,

you will feel them racing through
your whole body carrying
electrical signals saying

holy shit this
really is

The fucking shit
for me.

that scary man
—o—o—o—
being one
to disconnect from
due to being too
potent or
too pungent;
too subjective, sure,
what's left behind, though, is
less purulent now, with
subjective life back
at knifepoint,
piercing through my soul's
subcutaneous tissue
as a tease;
the leak
issues
non-submissives. I am
not leaving.

there's nowhere else
to go

outside of

high school's
stupidity traps

religion's twenty-four hour
snare drum attacks

failing relationships
that shouldn't have begun

money
always wanting to be number one

family
not leaving and leaving and not
not leaving but leaving again

getting and keeping this
one job that will please keep

                a roof
            over my head and

        alcoholic abandon...
        without knowing how...
        to let go of...
                        more alcohol

            being shucked-off
                by everyone important, dying.

writing.

the one, tasting right answer that has
not
        left
            yet;

at last.

<u>third base - not home yet</u>
I'm not sure when that happened.
going from pretty much always
feeling that
life didn't need me, anyway, and wondering
how long it would have to be
before-I'd-just-fucking-die-already,
counting on the fact of that happening.
knowing that in death,
as in good sex,
I join legions of bottoms just waiting,
with my own special ways to tease;
death, taking charge of the situation,
some day,
throwing my ass to the floor and getting busy.
it's gonna happen.
true for everyone waiting here in line with me,
eventually.
either the doorbell will ring,
or you-know-who will crawl
through an opened window or I'll be pushed
into the back seat of a smashed car
here now, whispering my name,
making me really feel seen and

that one kind of
you-know-what-heat
being ravaged.

I don't even remember when
or how
it happened that
I let go

of that
long-time-ago fantasy,
and found
myself; wanting to live, but
shit, some days...

that first love

be true enough

to believe it'll last forever.

this day did all of this.
all on its own.
lived the poem before it was written
leaving the writing
for tomorrow
in ink, but today, we will say
thank you to the invisible
everything present
that yes,
is already here, with its own
handwritten poem;
interlacing
with this single page.

(not giving my)
        too weak notice
_____o___o___o___

arriving at what would be
an aggressively unacceptable
departure time, I am
left to respectfully notify all
friends and colleagues that
I will not be leaving,
incredible as this might seem,
actively denying all outward
attempts at forced
passivity; growth,
I won't be going away. instead,
here with the steadfast
reminder that it will be
me, giving my best
at the next
not-a-sermon;
heaven's renewal, gathering

our purple church of Jesus ...
    ... because I remain
deployable
with my new employer.
any pre-set times for departure
    are for God to decide;
my job requirements provide
the strength
and the will
... to be here
    in this exact time for this...
one moment of renewal.

untangling:: —
one more
death that keeps on dying
again, landing me ready-made
at its front door
to brush off my life's
        road-grit feet welcome mat
index finger
        hovering
over a doorbell while looking
through
        texturized glass
        reassembling
        fractured-humanoid puzzle-shapes,
most of them keeping me stuck
in my own skin, because
        who knows who they are
        when they're always made-to-be blurry
with
memories' built-ins;
        the mechanical life-safeties of our histories
since the moment that... they had all died.
                        all of them...
                        all of them...

until, finally...
pushing the hear-it-this-time button
ringing
        today it's my turn
                to be done.

101

what I love about poets
is that we don't
motherfucking stop, because
we just cannot;
stop
hearing clear rhythms from the inside
of jars full of fermenting honey.
it's motherfucking everywhere that we go
so much so we don't
know any method of escape
from what,
for us, is
being the only human being around
who is hearing this sound
of Excalibur being happy-jizzed
while getting pulled out of a rock;
on us to somehow describe
weilding it high-high-high enough to tickle
Gods fuzzy belly-button, justalittle...then
hearing Her-Holiness bust-out with laughter;
that is our only option.
splattering flashing words opened
against hard surfaces to examine
the disassembled syllables...

...

that juice has gotta come from somewhere,
for a poet, caught standing in the rapids
without hip-boots amidst another
mid-river catch-and-release;
being the bait...
leaving everything
here, where
nothing is over,
again.

51425

when

where you've been
wants to pretend
it determines
for you
where
you're
going
next... and
forever,
it's
important
imp
for
you

(at the very
least)

to
pay
attention.

<u>why do you care?</u>

no,
really.
I'm asking you.
Feel free
to write your
best answer or two
to that, somewhere to look at,
along with whatever it is
you are doing
and still plan to do
about any of that. In fact,
write it everywhere.

The World's Greatest Bodybuilders

Guess who showed up for you
    on that one day that you wished
        you could someday forget.
Nurses. And guess who was there,
    standing right next to you, ready with
washed hands
        wearing thin plastic gloves just
    minutes after you'd said to your friends
    "hold my beer." Nurses.
Who knew what to say to you
        when your doctors all left you with
more questions you ever knew you could have;
        your nurses. Who could go
from stat labs to stat vomit bags
    in under two seconds, who would
stuff gauze, without blinking, into
places that you couldn't... or wouldn't...
    ever want to see, then returning,
        just a little bit later   to wipe
        those private places that
you just couldn't

quite reach.
all cleaned up now
with a fresh, warm blanket and your
call light right next to you.
who kept you safe
    through your seizures
    helped you feel less afraid
of what you were so afraid of, and who
stayed with you if or when,
                God forbid,
            you had lost
        so much blood... or maybe,
        all consciousness, or
who was it that
kept that from happening in the first place
remembering, at the same time,
the patient next door wants another
        sandwich; just one more
        minute, gotta get this
        ECG, another round of orthostatics
        and report
for the next patient who is on the way

while no matter what, guess who
    spent whatever
      extra time that it took to let you know
      that
      they-could-see-you
      when you
      couldn't even remember
      the last time that
      you-had-felt-seen
        before this.
nurses.

and just one more
  guess-what-else; this one:
who shows up for your nurse
  when your nurse has juggled
    each one of your needs, multiplied by
    at least
      each one of their patients with
their best, semi-fresh patience & grace
    between every other
queazy-quazi-catastrophe or legit threat
  including, yes,

dodging bodily fluids thrown with abandon,
  cringeworthy insults with fists, or
    another of those,
not anywhere close to being as delightful
  as they think; hose-monsters
    with their gross-pervert advances.

  not kidding.

wrangling twelve hours
spent turning new patients through
  new rooms cleaned just seconds ago,
  nearly always with
    a fresh smile and a greeting, but without
eating or pooping or peeing or even just seeing
  some sunlight...
    when they really need to...just stop,
    for a minute or two;
  guess who shows up for that.
  your nurse's buddy-nurse friend for the day,
    jumping right in
      before your nurse flames out.
That's who
      is able to see your nurse...

109   - - - - - 4 - - - -

the same way that your nurse

sees you...

...saying, don't you worry about all of that
just now.

your only job... right now,

is to just rest for a minute.

I gotchu fam, for real.

who

does

that?

Nurses. That's who.

for my homemade Mom ♡

Evelyn · Cherie · Marie-Edith

Angela · Elise

Jenna Hidalgo · Erin · Sarah · Cindy

Roselle · Gisèle · Zo · Melody

Hilary · Chuck · Bren · Meredith

The Best SARAH · Ma Hailey · Allison · Nicole · Portia

Amelia · Julia Jams · Mandy · Kylee

Sammy · Kwumymma

111

Worthiness is always
            purchased As Is.
There are exactly zero
        goddamn-corporation-religions'
          tithed-guarantees needed.

You and I are not a part of anyone's
   bottom-line to be heaven-made through

management approval
baptismal
renewal;
      fire sale-used product-liquidation
                  (just missing some

torn-off parts.)

            God

ain't gonna waste anyone's time
      attempting to haggle for better goods
   with greased-up middle-men or any

glint-toothed
soul grifters making bets.

wrong number

don't let anyone tell you that
    while you are praying the right way
you must be dialing the wrong number
    if you're not hearing what they have said
the right answer should be.

you will know God's voice is
    for you
    when you are hearing and knowing
        you are being heard with

what you know
are your
authentic ears...

        that is how you begin
to listen

from your own unlisted phone booth.

you don't plan
      for the end of the world
you plan
      for the world to be
continuing; doing what you are
       doing and seeing
what you see every day

the same way, because
        this time,
        right at this moment,
is all of the time in the world.

                        — for Cody

seeing
     today is
   this is our dream. closing our
      sometimes eyes...there is nowhere
    I need to hide
  to be here when the rest of life's sentence is
    ...flittering
                in this...
scurry-about marathon spent scattering
  ashes of flattened impermanence;
    sparks into dust... this glorious
      impermeable firmament
spraying rain when it's time; brazen
     as fuck
        with purpose
               and patience
                    impertinent how
   ...it just waits with wet eyes
bringing me inside, through   front door
                      truth & illusion's
landing, unlocked with exhilerating lips;
warmth and wailing felt through finger tips
  lighting the generous sky while gliding
  through every corner of delicious
    exile.

...then, the moon
and the trees
said to me

"don't worry, fam,
we got you!"

... your last words
EVER;
on your mark,
get set,
GO!

...

...

...

...

...

...

...

118